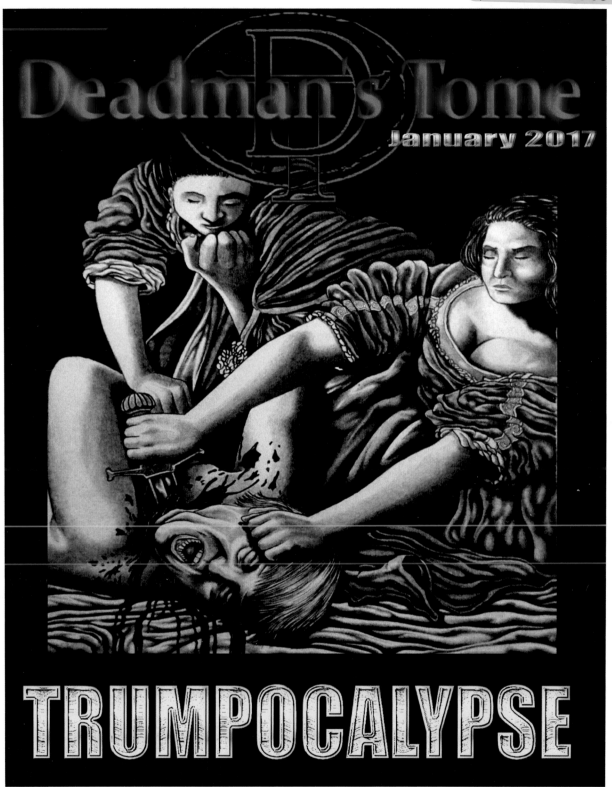

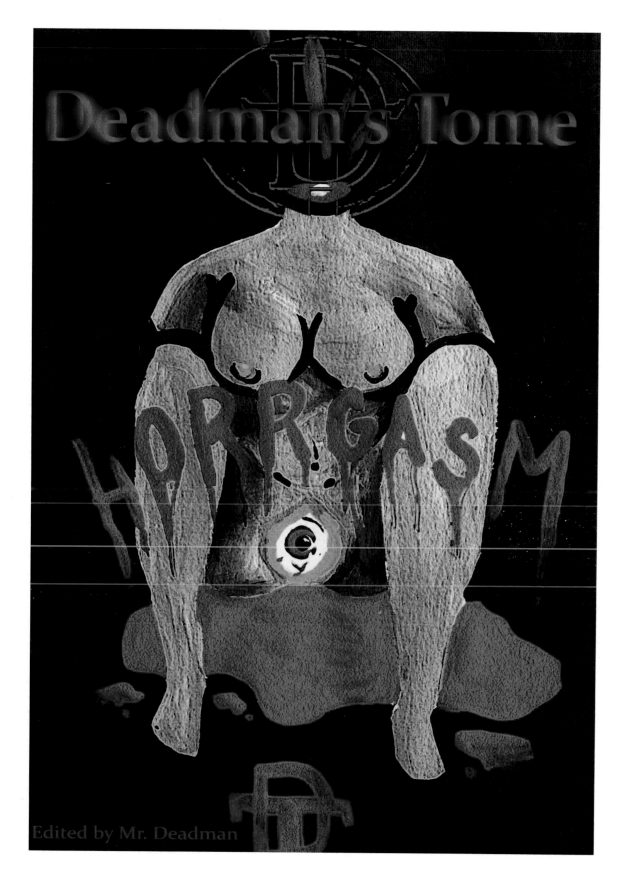

Deadman's Tome

HORRGASM

Edited by Mr. Deadman

NASTY
Fetish Fights Back

Introduction

"People love me. And you know what, I have been very successful. Everybody loves me." - Donald Trump

People love you, alright. But not in the way you think, Mr. Get-Rich-Off-Of-Daddy's-Tit. People love to mock you. People love to shower you with disrespect. If it was an option, people would drop a steaming pile of sloppy feces on your name. When you pass away, people would line up just to piss on your grave. But that wouldn't matter to you, would it? The golden showers would come at a price, and boy would people fork over the cash. Regardless, you are the president of the United States of America, and I will raise a glass to you and give you that much. I" call you President, but with it comes a whole nasty serving of unadulterated ridicule. This issue of Deadman's Tome is all about you, Mr. Trump. Dark, twisted, satirical tales at your expense, plus with a interview you had with me that you may not recall. I hope you enjoy.

Let it be known, I don't care where you are politically. I don't care if you are the biggest Hillary supporter or a giant Trump supporter. What I care about is doing the right thing by having fun at the President's expense, calling out his bull, and in the process create an issue where through laughter and pain we can begin to heal. This issue of Deadman's Tome starts with an interview with horror writer S. J. Budd, which is followed by an interview with Donald Trump. That's right, Donald Trump called me one night over Skype. He does this on a regular basis. He wants Deadman's Tome to bust his balls, get him red, and make him cry. The Frog Soldiers and Hell to Pay put the the Donald's Twitter behavior on blast. The Appointment turns cabinet selection into a battle royale. Donald's Drop showcases the routine executions. I Have a Very Good Brain takes us to a possible apocalyptic endgame scenario. Fired Works brings out the Founding Fathers to cast judgment and illustrate that they are not the shining examples of humanity like many would have you believe. Warhawk is the fate of the world depending on the power of two tiny hands, and Rat and Miriam paints life in a wasteland after all the fallout had settled.

Table of Contents

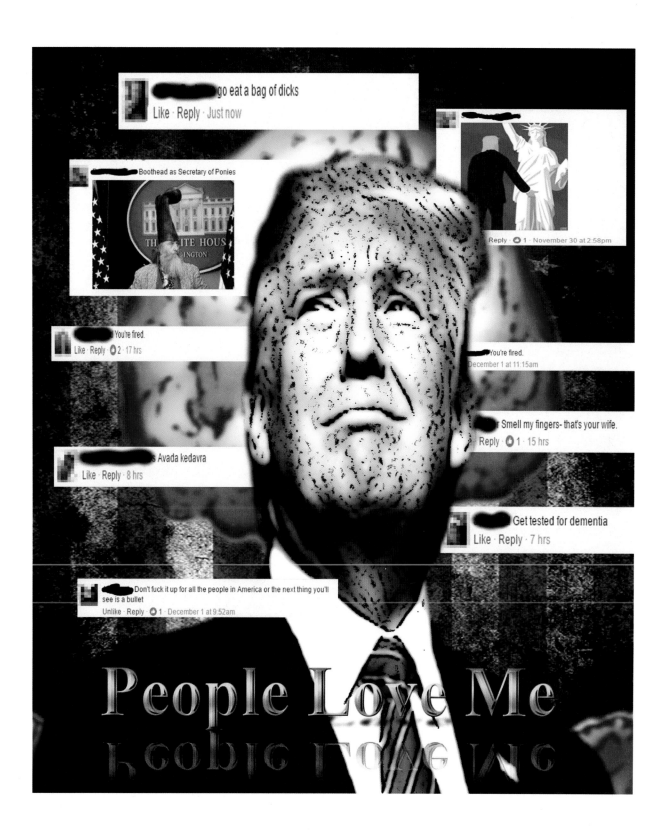

...go eat a bag of dicks
Like · Reply · Just now

Boothead as Secretary of Ponies

Reply · 1 · November 30 at 2:58pm

You're fired.
Like · Reply · 2 · 17 hrs

You're fired.
December 1 at 11:15am

...Smell my fingers- that's your wife.
Reply · 1 · 15 hrs

...s Avada kedavra
Like · Reply · 8 hrs

Get tested for dementia
Like · Reply · 7 hrs

Don't fuck it up for all the people in America or the next thing you'll see is a bullet
Unlike · Reply · 1 · December 1 at 9:52am

People Love Me

Interview with S. J. Budd

S. J. Budd is a horror writer that has been featured twice on Deadman's Tome. Check out The Memory Chamber and Hold Me Tight.

Q1) For those that don't know, who is S J Budd?

Hi my name is Sarah Budd a.k.a S.J.Budd. I now live in London but I spent my childhood and formative years growing up in my native birthplace, Cornwall. To me Cornwall is a very special place which to this day still retains its Celtic roots. I've always thought of it as a magical place and after all it is the home of Tintagel Castle where King Arthur himself was supposedly conceived. I grew up listening to Cornish legends of mermaids, strange beasts which roam the Cornish moors, pixies, pirates, witches and of course lots and lots of ghosts. This had a big effect on me as I grew up and I've always been fascinated with the other realms of the world we live in.

Q2) When did you know you wanted to be a writer?

It's all I've ever wanted to be. I've always liked to write even when I was very small so I guess it's just in my blood. What I really love about writing is making up characters and seeing the world through a different pair of eyes. I really like getting into character and being someone else for a few hours. People around me say I live in a dream world and it's true!
Writing is something I've done all my life but after getting my first job I decided to give it a real go and see how far I could take it. I was working in an office and just found it all terribly dull

and needed something to relieve my boredom and keep myself sane. Plus if it works out, I'll won't have to spend the rest of my life photocopying and making tea. My ultimate dream as a writer is to be able to just spend all day writing.

Q3) Why Horror? Where there significant works of horror, film or literature, that inspired you?

I think the film that started my passion with writing was Jim Henson's The Labyrinth. I must have first seen it when I was very little and I was just like wow! I never knew such worlds existed and it ignited in me a lifelong love of fantasy and horror. It may not seem a scary film now but as a six year old, when I first saw it I was terrified of those goblins and their Goblin King!

I've always loved horror because I like how you can get really scared by something such as a book or a film but in a safe environment. I love being creeped out and for me a great story is one that lingers on in your mind long after you've stopped reading it. One of the creepiest and disturbing films I've seen in a long time was The Mist by the epic master of horror, Stephen King. (Warning! Major spoiler alert for those who haven't seen it.) I have to confess, I haven't read the book, but watching the film was terrifying, especially at the end when David the main character feels he has no option other than to kill his beloved child humanely to prevent him from being eaten by killer bugs. However moments after killing his son, out of love thinking they were all about to die, he is miraculously saved much to his horror for it meant he killed his son for nothing and now has to live without him. For me that is true horror!

Q4) The Labyrinth is an amazing and bizarre film, for sure. Tell me, how was your first experience with the film?

For me watching The Labyrinth was unlike anything I had ever seen before. It was a story in which everything was turned on it's head. It was just so creative and there were no clear cut good guys and bad guys which made for really interesting characters. I think it showed me that there are no limits to one's imagination.

Q5) You mentioned The Mist, a great Stephen King story that was turn into a movie with a divided audience, but the ending was arguably one of the best moments: the strange giant beasts, the message that humanity could prevail, but not without first tormenting the main character with an overpowering sense of dread. How has this inspired your writing?

Yeah, I guess I quite like that about horror in that there can be an overall happy ending, but not for everyone. I think even in horror there has to be some sort of uplifting scene at the end. I think what's inspired me most about my writing with regards to Stephen King is that he said his stories are all based on the same formula. In that he takes a bunch of characters and places them in a ridiculous situation and simply watches it all unfold. I've written a few stories like that and it's a really fun way of writing as not even you know what is going to happen.

Q6) What was your inspiration behind The Memory Chamber?

The inspiration for The Memory Chamber, was the notion that memories can change with time. Sometimes something awful can happen but then years later you can look back and laugh. But of course it works the other way round, that really happy memories can be the most painful reminders of what you once had.

Q7) Are there memories you would pay to forget? Would be willing to share?

No not at all, because without the bad memories how would you appreciate the good ones? I think memories are there for us to learn from and often the painful ones hold a lesson for us.

Q8) What was your inspiration behind Hold Me Tight?

I've long been fascinated with ghosts, with the idea that these were once people who were so damaged in life that they are unable to move on even after they've died. I had this idea of someone being wronged that they hated their perpetrator even after death.

Q9) Did anyone ever tell you that Hold Me Tight comes to mind whenever they have a drink?

No, not until now!

Q10) What is your best accomplishment as a writer?

I think it has to be when I had my first short story published in issue 28 of Sanitarium Magazine. I was so over the moon as I had been writing for some time but was getting nowhere and to have my first story published was an amazing feeling.

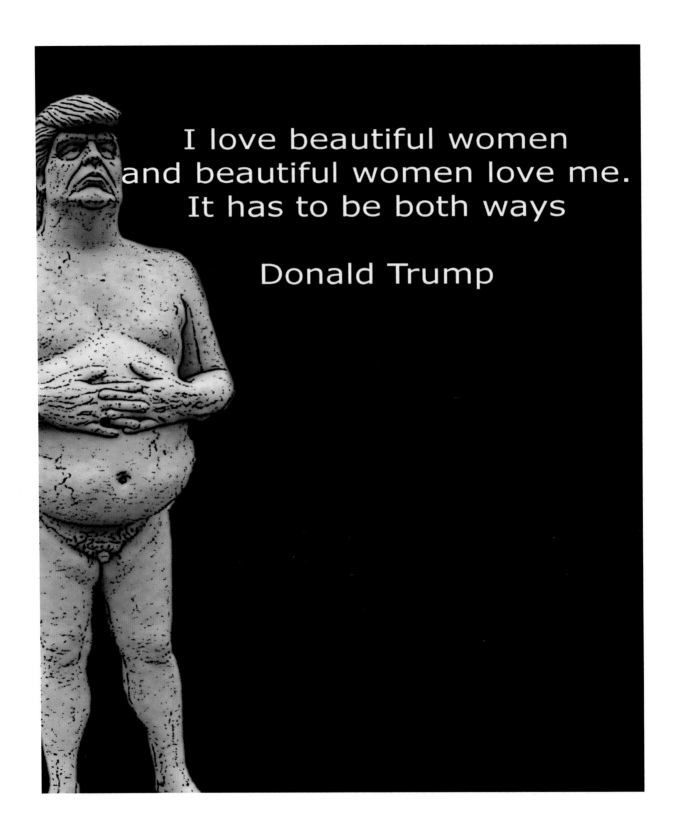

I love beautiful women
and beautiful women love me.
It has to be both ways

Donald Trump

Interview with Donald Trump

Donald Trump may deny this up and down, and you may find this hard to believe, but the orange faced baboon agreed to meet with me via Skype over an encrypted line. He assured me that the Russians would make sure no one would ever find proof of our connection to protect his presidency. They need him. The world needs him., or so he claims. But why would Donald Trump choose Deadman's Tome for an interview? Ah, because every one, even Trump, has his soundboard, his emotional ground, his mental wash. A person that one can confess sins without consequence, like a priest. Like I said, Donald Trump may deny this interview ever existed, but believe me, these words are most certainly his. But this interview is a work of fiction and just a jab at the President's ego.

1) **How's it going Donald. It's okay that I still call you Donald after winning the presidency and all, right?**

"You know, it really doesn't matter what the media write, as long as you've got a young and beautiful piece of ass."

2) **Uh, thank you? Are you ready to be the president?**

"I will be the greatest jobs president that God ever created."

3) **God, huh? That's a pretty tall order, what makes you think you can do that?**

"I think the only difference between me and the other candidates is that I'm more honest and my women are more beautiful."

4) **Can't lie that you do seem to surround yourself with beautiful women. How are things with Ivanka?**

"I did try and fuck her... I moved on her like a bitch, but I couldn't get there."

5) You're own daughter? You've tried to fuck your own daughter? You sure that's a good idea?

"That may be the best idea of all. I would say I'm the all-time judge, don't forget, I own the Miss Universe pageant."

6) Do you normally have hit on your daughter?

"Haven't we all...are we babies?"

7) Uh...

"I just start kissing them. It's like a magnet. Just kiss. I don't even wait. And when you're a star, they let you do it. You can do anything. Grab them by the pussy. You can do anything."

8) Donald... I don't think we can still have this conversation. I mean, I understand that you come to me as your soundboard and all, but you know I can't support this.

"My fingers are long and beautiful, as, it has been well documented, are various other parts of my body."

9) Wait, are you sending me... You just sent me a pic of your dick, you fucking bastard. Why did you dick pic me?

"I take advantage of the laws of the nation."

10) Donald, I'm so close to blocking you. Is there something else on your mind.

"I believe [the media] like making me out to be something more sinister than I really am."

11) How so?

"I don't want the Presidency. I'm going to help a lot of people with my foundation–and for me, the grass isn't always greener."

12) Donald, you told me before you were a Hillary plant, but that things went out of control. What happened?

"We can't continue to allow China to rape our country"

13) Uh, okay... I think we're about done here, Donald. You have a closing statement?

"How stupid are the people of Iowa?"

The Frog Soldiers

@MichaelJEpstein

@realDonaldTrump 20 Jan 2017 DNA mods will begin immediately for our men of the armed forces. I mean the women too, but remember when they didn't mind being called men.

@realDonaldTrump 20 Jan 2017 So many losers spreading lies about DNA mods! Twitter is failing because they let the losers in! Sad!

@realDonaldTrump 21 Jan 2017 I have sent forces to seize the offices of Twitter. This will now be the official, national communication channel. No more ISIS tweets!

@realDonaldTrump 21 Jan 2017 Obama had 8 years to stop ISIS and sad losers from tweeting. Shameful!

@realDonaldTrump 23 Jan 2017 DNA mixing problems is a Chinese hoax! We are saving MONEY! Crooked scientists just want grants!

@realDonaldTrump 30 Jan 2017 @jeffreygoldblum your research is garbage. Who cares what you think about super soldiers & frog DNA. American people have given a mandate.

@realDonaldTrump 11 Apr 2017 failing @CNN just wants their reporters to grow extra limbs like our soldiers. Losers! Shame!

@realDonaldTrump 20 Apr 2017 So many liars! Army is not rebelling. I am the commander! I just spoke to @GeneralAnura. Great guy.

@realDonaldTrump 21 Apr 2017 .@GeneralAnura and the frog men can have Texas. We don't want it anyway. No jobs. Pathetic!

@realDonaldTrump 1 May 2017 Those nuclear devices were just going to waste in the warehouse. @GeneralAnura is no longer serving. That's what happens to traitors!

@realDonaldTrump 2 May 2017 So many beautiful pictures of the sky on fire. Radioactive fallout is gorgeous. Just terrific. Forget the haters!

@realDonaldTrump 7 May 2017 couldn't be happier that the frog men are now 20 ft tall. ISIS has no frog soldiers! I am a very smart guy. The smartest.

@realDonaldTrump 8 May 2017 @algore shame on you. Apologize! @GeneralAnura is a great guy. A 20 ft great guy. Just terrific.

@realDonaldTrump 11 May 2017 The frog soldiers eat mosquitos and fight ISIS. No more terrorists. No more Zika! Which was a hoax anyway! America is becoming great.

@realDonaldTrump 15 May 2017 We are building a wall. It's the best wall ever built. All around Trump Tower. A frog proof wall. The best wall you've ever seen.

@realDonaldTrump 21 May 2017 Real Americans all join the effort to drain the swamps. The frog soldiers cannot attack without water nearby. Losers!

@realDonaldTrump 24 May 2017 Crooked Hillary gave the frog men water. As soon as this is over, I am going to launch an investigation. Shameful! She's the puppet.

@realDonaldTrump 29 May 2017 We built the best wall. We made the frog men pay for it. They can't get in.

@realDonaldTrump 29 Jun 2017 No electricity for a month thanks to EPA regulations the frog men imposed. My daughter is very beautiful by candlelight. What a killer body!

@realDonaldTrump 4 July 2017 We celebrate America today! BBQ frog legs are delicious. Just terrific. The only American soldiers who died were losers anyway.

@realDonaldTrump 21 July 2017 Frog men keep saying frog people. Political correctness! Remember when giant radioactive mutants were called mutant men and no one cried?

@realDonaldTrump 27 July 2017 Frog MEN told me to give up the country. Sad! Crooked generals. Called Putin. A real man. Not a frog man. Terrific guy.

@realDonaldTrump 1 Aug 2017 Spoke with Russians. Spoke with China. They congratulated me on killing the frogs. They are going to join in making America frog free.

@realDonaldTrump 2 Aug 2017 Purple night sky across USA beautiful. The best neutron bombs everywhere. All of the buildings are just great. Trump Tower, still terrific.

@realDonaldTrump 4 Aug 2017 Americans still alive, I have so many jobs for you. Contracted rebuilding of America to Trump Construction Enterprises. Fantastic company!

@realDonaldTrump 21 Aug 2017 Made a deal with frog people. They won't kill and eat all of America, but we just need to make everything into a swamp, which is terrific.

@realDonaldTrump 22 Aug 2017 Lazy Congress tried to halt the swamp. Frog people ate them. Sad! Losers!

@realDonaldTrump 30 Aug 2017 These frog DNA injections are fabulous. Never felt so good in my life.

@realDonaldTrump 2 Sept 2017 We have a shortage of flies. @jeffreygoldblum, how is your research coming?

Donald J. Trump
@realDonaldTrump

Sorry losers and haters, but my I.Q. is one
of the highest -and you all know it! Please
don't feel so stupid or insecure,it's not your
fault

RETWEETS 10,922 FAVORITES 8,514

6:37 PM - 8 May 2013

Hell to Pay

Kelly Evans

It all started with a twitter conversation. What seemed to be a meeting of the mutual appreciation society quickly turned nasty. The American President Donald J Trump offered a heartfelt compliment to the North Korean dictator Kim Jong Un.

 Donald J. Trump @realdonaldtrump

@kimjongun seems like a really great guy, his people think he's terrific. Maybe the US should take notes…

⇆200 ♥ 1.6k

After a flurry of unnecessarily sensationalist media attention, the supreme leader replied with praise of his own.

Chairman, Supreme Leader @kimjonun

@realdonaldtrump Congrats on your win, you're just what America needs right now. Looking forward to working with you. #newBFF?

↰⇄16.3m ♥ 20.4m

 PRESIDENT Donald J. Trump @realdonaldtrump

@kimjungun Yes, lots to talk about. #oristhere

↰⇄34 ♥ 2.3k

 Chairman, Supreme Leader, Powerful Man @kimjonun

@realdonaldtrump We should meet up, face to face. I will allow it. #benevolence

↰⇄13.4m ♥ 18.6m

 PRESIDENT, Successful Businessman Donald J. Trump @realdonaldtrump

@kimjungun I'm a very busy man, very important man, rich, but I'm sure something can be arranged. #mypeoplewillcallyourpeople

⤵4.5k ♥ 3k

 Chairman, Supreme Leader, Benevolent to All @kimjonun

@realdonaldtrump You should come to my country, I'll introduce you to my barber. #betterthanyours #kiddingnotkidding

⤵18.9m ♥ 17.9m

 Chairman, Supreme Leader, Benevolent to All @kimjonun

@realdonaldtrump And my wife will show #Melania where a supreme leader's wife shops. #versace #dior

⤵15.6m ♥ 13.7m

Trump's account went silent for a few days, after which new tweets began to appear.

 PRESIDENT, Multi-Millionaire Donald J. Trump @realdonaldtrump

That @kimjongun guy, knows nothing about me or my wife. Foolish to assume.

⤵7.6k ♥ 5.6k

PRESIDENT, Multi-Millionaire Donald J. Trump @realdonaldtrump

The corrupt and lying media think they know what's going on. They don't. #southkorea

↰ 88.7k ♥ 1.1m

 PRESIDENT, Multi-Millionaire Donald J. Trump @realdonaldtrump

I don't need your barber, @kimjungun, mine is terrific, visits me at #trumptower whenever I want. #erniethebarber

↰ 76k ♥ 69k

♥ Big Papa Bear @vladimirputin retweeted your tweet.

22h: I don't need your barber, @kimjungun, mine is terrific, visits me at #trumptower whenever I want. #erniethebarber

69k other likes

 PRESIDENT, Multi-Millionaire Donald J. Trump @realdonaldtrump

@kimjungun Kim Fatty the Third - looks like HE is where all the food in #southkorea is going #whoateallthepies

↰ 1.2m ♥ 1.3m

 PRESIDENT, Multi-Millionaire Donald J. Trump @realdonaldtrump

Once again the media are lying about me. I am not in secret talks with China. #southkorea #kimfattyIII

↰ 2.3m ♥ 2.1m

 Chairman, Supreme Leader, Benevolent to All @kimjonun

@realdonaldtrump Your comments are…puzzling. #fingeronthebutton

↰ 16.8m ♥ 15.9m

 PRESIDENT, Multi-Millionaire Donald J. Trump @realdonaldtrump

@kimjonghun Nothing 'puzzling' about me, I tell it like I see it, got me elected. What's puzzling is why we haven't seen your wife in public for a while. #justsayin'

↰ 45k ♥ 1.2m

Family Man, Supreme Leader, Benevolent to All @kimjonun

@realdonaldtrump My family is not your concern. #potkettleblack

⤴ ⇄21.2m ♥ 22.5m

PRESIDENT, Multi-Millionaire Donald J. Trump @realdonaldtrump

People are telling me, smart people, terrific people, that @kimjongun did away with his wife. I don't know if it's true, but people are saying. #listening

⤴ ⇄67k ♥ 98k

PRESIDENT, Multi-Millionaire Donald J. Trump @realdonaldtrump

People are saying 'Donald, why do you say such things? Don't you know he has nukes?' Nukes? Those tiny rockets he uses for fishing? 1/2

⤴ ⇄1.1m ♥ 2m

PRESIDENT, Multi-Millionaire Donald J. Trump @realdonaldtrump

2/2 I tell it like it is, we have free speech in America and it's terrific. Except the media, they're a bunch of liberal lyin' losers. I'm not afraid of an overgrown asian weeble.

⇄2.5m ♥ 3.1m

The next day the bombs fell. President Trump was airlifted from Trump Tower and taken to a secure location, along with surviving members of his cabinet. Despite there being no wifi or electricity, the president refuses to surrender his mobile device, still tweeting to an audience no longer listening.

End

The Appointment

Philip W. Kleaver

She lost her breath when she hit the coffee table. Her chin cracked against the smooth mahogany and she bit the inside of her lip, drawing blood. She could sense the man looming over her, and she rolled to her left, landing on the carpet. Her chest rose and fell irregularly. The man smiled. He straightened his tie and stepped forward.

"I got you now, bitch."

She drew in air through her nostrils, trying to steady herself. She waited… waited… and brought her leg up, driving the sharp point of her scarpin heel (a sensible royal blue) into the man's crotch. He retched and his knees buckled. She crawled backwards; the carpet left little burns on her elbows and calves (she *knew* she should have worn pantyhose, but had thought a flash of leg might help her chances). The back of her head thumped against soft upholstery. She stood up, using the plush chair for support.

The man staggered towards her, still hunched over. His face was twisted in hatred. She thought of all the times she had seen that look: when she corrected a male classmate on the finer points of the law, when she had ascended to head of her department and gave instructions to desk jockeys with patchwork whiskers, hell, even when she committed the sin of denying a man a date. It gave her a sudden strength, like a shot of good bourbon. He had more brute strength, yes, but she was smarter and more agile. She lashed at him with her nails, leaving deep red trenches in his cheek, and ran toward the other end of the room.

She wobbled on her heels, tore them off, and hurled them at the man. He dodged one, swatted the other. He chuckled. She stood with her back to the curved wall, her muscles tight. The man lunged. She feinted right and stepped left, but the man threw out his hand and grabbed her hair. She yelped and whipped her head violently away from him. There was a sound like tearing paper. The man looked down at a fistful of blonde hair. She could feel tendrils of heat on down her cheek. Her blood dripped down, staining the carpet with small, perfect circles.

"Won't look too good in the official portrait now," the man taunted. "Lucky I can spare you the embarrassment."

He lunged again, his hands outstretched towards her throat. She couldn't help it--she screamed. He forced his thumbs into her windpipe, cutting off the sound. She beat at his face and neck, but he ignored her blows. She stumbled backwards, slamming into a bookshelf. A few leather-bound volumes hit the ground. Darkness crept in from the edge of her vision. She felt lightheaded. The man's eyes narrowed, and the corners of his mouth rose in a wicked grin. Her hands scrabbled at the shelves behind her, until her fingers hit something cold and metallic.

She brought the object around in a wide arc, striking the man just above his brow. He shouted in pain. She struck again, and his hands jerked away from her neck to cover the gash in his forehead. His eyes had the confused, dull look of a drunk trying to pull open a locked door. She shoved him, sending his body to the floor with a crash. She straddled his chest and brought her weapon down again and again. She thought of all the men who had stood in her way before, claiming superiority simply because of chromosomal chance.

"FUCK YOU!"

She heard the crunch of his skull breaking, but still she attacked. There was a sickening squelch, like a boot being pulled out of deep mud, as she raised her weapon out of the mess of blood, brains, and bone that was once the man's face. She let it drop beside him--a bronze statue of an eagle, coated in gore.

A slow clap came from the other side of the room. She glanced up and met the gaze of the president. From behind his imposing desk, he shifted his weight and touched the tips of his short fingers together. He seemed affable, his face like that of a man who had just heard a good joke.

"Terrific! Look, I've seen a lot of these lately, okay? A lot of fights, with a lot of very, very good fighters, terrific fighters. This was one of the best, believe me. Come over here, sweetheart." His voice was pinched, punctuated with sniffling.

She walked over towards the president's desk, shaking.

"And you've got a great figure, too, really high class. Beautiful. I love beautiful women. Come shake my hand, sweetheart."

The president rose and stuck out his hand, which seemed too small for his shirtsleeve. She put her bloodstained hand in his. The other crept around to cup her ass.

"Congratulations, Miss Staff Secretary. You earned it. I know you'll do a great job. The best. Why don't you go clean yourself up? Make yourself look great again."

The president winked, then leaned over and pressed a button on his desk.

"Send someone in here to get this piece-of-shit loser off my floor. Get my tailor on the line, too. I want something new to wear to the Secretary of State battle royale. It's big league."

Thank you, Putin

Donald's Drop

Joey Whiston

He had stopped using an alarm clock weeks ago; the morning executions served that purpose well enough. He now woke refreshed, knowing that it was business-as-usual in the greatest place on earth.

Crossing the room, the man stopped briefly before the windows and cracked open the heavy red curtains. In the courtyard, the line of *criminals* who had, only moments before, received their due punishments were being cleared away, ready for a fresh batch. Sensitive to the morning light and not yet equipped with contact lenses, his eyes could not make out who was being sentenced today. *Immigrants or queers? Terrorists or protesters?* The curtain fell back into place, and he decided it didn't really matter. *They'll all feel the American Dream soon enough, oh yes sir.*

The next round of *cracks* couldn't have come at a more perfect time; at the apex of his morning piss. He felt as if he could smell the gun smoke from the bathroom, and enjoyed the symbolism of his yellow fluids being flushed away until only pristine-white remained. Just three more batches were left that morning, and then his day would officially begin.

He faced the mirror. He was old now – *older*, anyway. A sudden thought then took him – he craned his head to the side, shifting the way the light hit his face, adding a couple more years.

It was still there, he could see it; the scar just below his ear lobe. Brief hesitation, then he ran his finger across it. His mind instantly lit up, like someone had rigged a flashbang to go off at the slightest touch of his old wound.

He's back in his house. Not his big, expensive New York house, or even his shore house, but his house-house. The one he grew up in, just by the countryside.

He's crying. A dark-skinned man had walked past the fence of the garden, startling him to such a degree that he had fallen off the slide and cut himself.

His mother had come rushing out then, all sweet smiles and shushing sounds. He explained between tears and hiccups what had happened – that a dark skinned man had scared him, and he had fallen.

"Why did he look so *different?!*" he had demanded of his mother. This part of the flashback was crystal clear, a white-hot portion of his memory.

"Don't be afraid, Donald" she had said,

"He's just like you."

After a few blinks, he was back at his sink; silk bathrobe admirably covering his soft flesh. His eyes were wide and fixed on themselves, taking in his own reflection but only seeing his mother's smile in the glass.

Then he heard the next round of gunshots. He even heard the resounding thuds of the bodies, falling as one. Before he could process it, he was out the bathroom door, through his bedroom and running down the hall. He heard himself screaming, but was too panicked to moderate or control himself. The doormen couldn't stop him, and soon his robe was flailing about in the morning breeze as he crossed the courtyard barefooted. The next round fired – and he saw it this time, making his screams louder and wilder.

All who saw him, all who *heard* him were in shock. As the rifles were loaded and aimed for the last time that day, the executioners saw their great leader pass in front of them suddenly, yelling out a single sentence over and over:

"They're just like us! THEY'RE JUST LIKE US!"

"I Have a Very Good Brain, and I've Said a Lot of Things

Patrick Winters

The meeting with the foreign dignitary had gone to shit long before the undead showed up, or at least that's what Adam Howell had thought. When he'd heard a groan come from the small crowd of onlookers attending the event, he'd assumed it was in response to the President's previous remark; when he heard the scream come after, though, he'd realized it was the sound of someone who'd just Turned.

Chaos had erupted in the room within a matter of seconds. More screams rose up as the crowd bolted in every direction. Adam and the other Secret Service agents rallied around the President, leading him straight on to the emergency exit. The sound of bodies falling, limbs tearing, and blood splashing on the floor began to interlace with the persisting cries of all-out fear.

The agents rushed the President out into the hall, the dignitary and his own men coming out behind them. They began dashing down the long way, brushing aside the clueless civilians in their path.

"We have a car waiting in the back of the building to get you out of here, Mr. President!" Palmer—the head of the team—shouted out.

"Great!" the President said, already huffing from his slow run. "That's great!"

A shrill, inhuman wail belted out from back in the conference room, followed by the racket of something being slammed into one of the walls.

"How the fuck did an infected person manage to get through security?" Matthews shouted from beside Adam. The other agent had pulled out his M&P 9 and was pointing it back down the hall. Adam drew his own and did the same—right as a wave of both normal and Turned people came rushing out towards them.

Adam had heard that the infection spread and changed people incredibly quickly, but he couldn't believe it could be *this* quick. Judging by their animalistic growls and their jarring movements, there were at least five people already Turned heading their way; and who knew who else had been bitten and could be Turning right that instant?

Howell opened fire first, and then Adam joined in, their bullets blasting by the dignitary and his men and towards the rapidly approaching crowd. Those who hadn't Turned tried ducking or falling to the floor to dodge the barrage, only to get trampled or bitten by the Turned among them. Adam took aim at a snarling, bloody-neck runner and put two shots into her chest; she stumbled but wouldn't go down, hissing and hacking angrily at him.

One of Howell's shots hit the visiting dignitary straight through the head; the politician's detail kept right on running as he fell to the ground.

"They're coming up fast!" Palmer hollered, and as the crowd of the Turned grew closer, Adam knew there was no escape; he, the agents, and the President wouldn't be able to outrun them.

Adam got off a few more shots before he ran out of ammo. As he set to ejecting and reloading, the bloodied woman he'd shot barreled into him. She brought him down to the ground and started tearing at his chest and his throat. He screamed and thought his last, rapid thoughts, one of which was: *I just died for a guy I didn't even vote for.*

And then he was gone.

Palmer and the other agents were overtaken as well, and just as quickly, leaving only Howell and the President left living in the hall. Howell charged off and ahead, leaving his Commander in Chief behind with a remorseless "Sorry, sir!"

The President let out a wild moan as he spared a glance behind him. He was terrified to see that one of the Turned was leaping right for him.

"B-- br-- brains!" it spat out in its frenzy.

The Turned fell upon the President, who let out a yell and tried shoving the crazed attacker off of him. It latched its jaws onto the tanned skin of his small hands, chomping down and rending flesh and cartilage away. Then it grabbed hold of his head and repeatedly slammed it into the ground, until the President moved and yelled no more.

The Turned viciously tore and clawed away at the man's scalp, tossing aside the bloodied mop of blonde hair once the brains were exposed. It licked its lips and sunk its fingers into the organ, pulling out chunks and stuffing them into its mouth. It chewed.

Its jaws slowed and the mad rage left its face.

It scrunched its nose in a sneer and stuck out its tongue, hacking out the foul-tasting gray and white matter.

"B-- brains," it choked out. "Bad . . . brains!"

With a mad howl, it rose up and darted off down the hall, looking for a better and fresher meal.

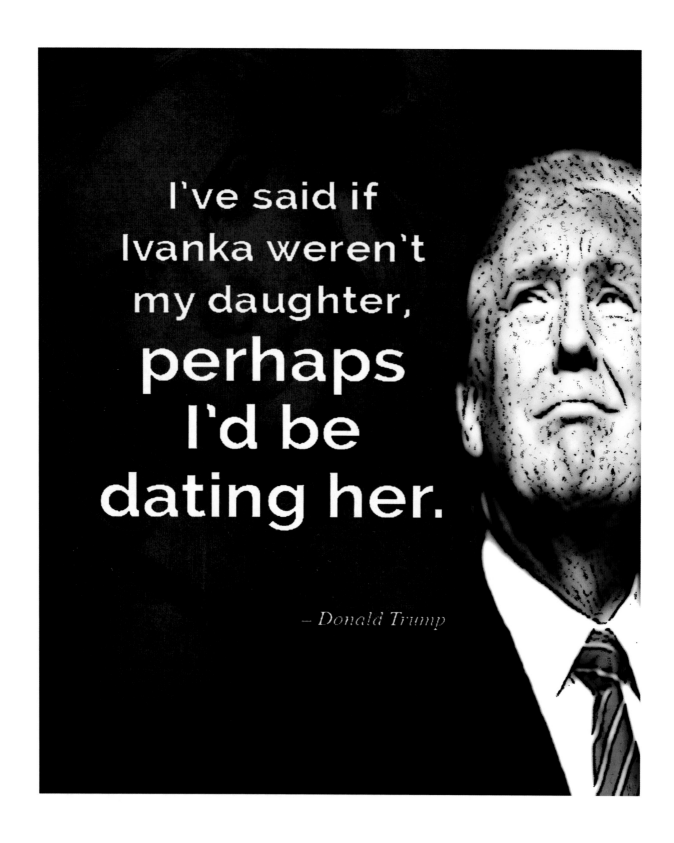

I've said if Ivanka weren't my daughter, **perhaps I'd be dating her.**

– *Donald Trump*

Fired Works

Erin Lee

Fact: *The original United States Declaration of Independence was signed on July 2, 1776. It didn't make the papers for two days. The old-school publishing delay may have made Fourth of July the official day of American independence, but the deaths of two of its creators sealed the bogus date forever. Disconcertingly, both US Presidents Thomas Jefferson and John Adams died on July 4 in 1826. Even more eerie is that they kicked the bucket five hours apart, with Jefferson passing first at age 82 and Adams at age 90. It wasn't planned that way, but it happened.*

(It's true, look it up).

Twisted, lesser known, fact: *The nation's founding duo cannot rest until they set history straight. They're pretty pissed off about it, and a few other things. After more than two dead duck centuries, they've had enough – especially in light of recent current events in a country they once loved. (They would have voted third party, had they been registered. They've decided,* *they should have rethought the electoral college). They've returned to America as ghost rebels Thomas and John – lame duck has-beens with amendments to make. This time, people will stand united or fall divided. That's the plan, anyway – for old time's sake. It's exactly what the people voted for...*

(Cue the fireworks).

***

Tis true: History's been transformed by a porker to the truth. Time has milled our intentions. Too much **crooked** progress. Too much—*what's the word?* —bling. Oh, and political correctness. We didn't have all the red, white and blue, feminism, or flashy pyrotechnics. That much, I do agree with the Ginger-At-Large on: No *woman* should be president.

That *(not a hot model, because those don't count)* immigrant in the white house with the bogus birth certificate making "change" and supporting minorities: Hell no! In our day, we celebrated democracy with greenery strung up by broads who knew their place. Common sense, if you ask me. But fear not: Love trumps hate. We founding fathers are near-term to fix things. **Believe me:** We have every intention of making **America** grope—**great**—**again**.

Maybe we should have anticipated it: #hindsight. *(Did I do that right? Somebody call Putin).* Still, it bothers us that we hold these truths—*lies really*—that we're one nation. What a bit. The *real* truth is that we've never been more divided. We can't even intercourse without censorship. And the media, **all lies**; just ask Agent Orange. ...Under *what* creator? Who is *he*? I haven't seen him—tis could never be a she—and I've been dead two centuries. The only guy making an appearance from time to time wears Mexican feather grass on his head: A sky rise built on Daddy's dime to heaven. Or hell? Somebody ought to **build a wall** around Manhattan. *(Pass the suction cups)*.

I told Abigail a million times that Independence Day would be the greatest day in history. I even made her write it down on parchment. She called me a dreamer and told me not to spend so much time with Tom. I ignored her, same as The Don does Mike. I really *did* believe, but the history books and a slow press made me into a liar. It's complete namby-pamby. Instead, all the hoopla goes to the inauguration of an Orange Wrecking Ball. (I hear there's going to be helicopters and Burnett's got front row seats between Bill's **nasty women**). Even now, she doesn't let me hear the end of it. I can't listen to that hussy for all eternity. She's worse than Megyn Kelly and Rosie combined and there's no dying of consumption when you're already dead. So, I'm going back, to manifest with Tom. We'll get our Independence Day…

This time, people will heed. And, I'm getting a drink; no Adam's Ale or sips of wine and crackers for me. *When in Russia, right?* I earned my guinea two hundred years over. I deserve it. I need it too: Women's liberation? The right to vote? Freedom of choice? Please! No one ever mentioned anything about jades and free speech. Tom spent months spelling it out for them: "We hold these truths to be self-evident, that all **men** are created equal, that they are endowed by their Creator with certain unalienable Rights." The key word, there, is men. Now, a man's intention isn't enough. It's 140 characters of #contempt. #greatagain? @nevertrump.

They've taken our vision and authored a mockery of our objectives. They've ignored the red of our blood. They've blemished our innocence and still call it white. And don't even talk to me about blue – the wall a reality TV star broke through. It's time to make things right. We have a few adjustments to make to our constitution. And we don't care who signs it. (They certainly didn't wait for *us* last time). Tom and I are **stronger together**. Tonight, we're giving the American people exactly what they voted for because when they go low, we go high.

***

November 9, 2016

High up on a hill, we watch her with her yellow hair hanging loose. *Begging to be grabbed, more like.* She points at fireworks set off as bland appetizers to the night pundits never saw coming. *Surprise, surprise!* **It was rigged. I promise you.** She laughs at the sparkler she can't light. *Dumb bitch. Probably voted* **crooked.** She twists her tongue around pink cloud candy on a stick. She smiles and licks her lips. Her name is Liberty. It's one of the reasons we picked her. She's the iconic beauty queen; nothing like **Miss Piggy**. We would know, we've watched her star-spangled bullshit for years.

We saw her the day she won homecoming queen and screwed not one, but three boys as thank-you's for votes. She speaks in short, choppy sentences: "Like," "Um," "Oh, wild." We watched her when she graduated, only a few short months ago. She wore a red cap and gown with a rhinestone mortar board reading 'Liberty for Prez, 2046.' *Yeah, sorry. Not happening.* She talked for exactly 112 minutes while the crowd yawned and wiped sweat from their eyes. She talked about everything and anything, but truth. She spoke of things no one will remember.

…But, fear not, great nation. *We* remember. Tonight, we'll *all* be free, watching Liberty take her justice. It is, after all, what you voted for. And **nobody likes a loser**.

***

Darkness falls. Fireworks shoot through the sky, lighting up the crowd and faces at Madison High School Alumni Field. They've come here with a plan. A soldier never goes off plan – not if he intends to win the war. A soldier always brings his **Mad Dog** along and never, ever gets caught.

"Look at that her, shaking her ass around like she owns the whole goddamn town. She's not even watching the stupid show," Thomas grumbles, taking a sip of beer. "Probably didn't even cast a vote." With a darkened sky, there's no reason to worry about open containers. *It's not like this land has had law and order for years.*

Liberty bounces and twirls, ignoring the show in the sky. She spins in circles with a young boy they can only assume is her brother. She calls him Samuel and gives him her last sparkler, telling him to be careful. The sky goes dark as she bends to light it – this time, without a hitch. Her round ass makes John pause before digging under the blanket for matching M16 rifles. He reaches into the bag and tosses a magazine to Thomas, grabs one for himself and slaps it into place. He looks to the sky—still dark—and decides it will only be seconds now. The crowd waits in anticipation for the final announcement.

Boom! **Boom!** *Bang!* **Boom!** *Pop!* Blazes of hot light crack darkness. Fireworks serge into the night. Luminescent explosions paint darkness in an array of reds, yellows, greens, and blues. Finally, the crowd takes their eyes off Liberty and transfixes on the pyrotechnics they came for, shouting "**lock her up!**"

Thomas raises his gun, pointing it toward Liberty.

John shakes his head. "Let's make her watch." He gestures toward Samuel. "Start with him."

Thomas raises the rifle and takes aim at the neon blue glow necklace around the kid's neck. He open fires, filling the young body with a short burst. The impact sends the boy off of his feet and to the ground in a bloody heap. Liberty doesn't notice. She's still spinning and laughing.

John laughs louder, taking aim at a broad who stands next to Liberty. ***Pop!*** He fires on her. The first round tears into her left tit, splattering blood over Liberty's gorgeous face. ***Pop. Pop. …Pop!***

Each blast is muffled by the fireworks as more and more bodies litter the field. Liberty is left alive among limp, lifeless remains and paralyzed. She isn't alone. The blood frenzy overtakes Thomas as he dry fires an empty weapon. He could barely get his bearings as John shakes him violently, handing him lit roman candles.

"Justice for all!" Thomas yells, shooting roman candles into the backs of people running from the bloody scene. People flee in every direction, some falling, as they are caught by blasts of fireworks and gunfire.

"Why?" She screams as tears cut through the blood coating her face. "Why?"

"Why?" John asks, with a sadistic smile. "…That's *exactly* what we want to know."

The duo open fires on Liberty, emptying their final magazines. Her gorgeous, flawless features are quickly defaced beyond recognition like a torn flag tossed in a dumpster behind a corporation. *I pledge allegiance…*

***

America, we made a few mistakes. You, our fellow Americans, have gotten a few things right, it seems. We are not afraid to admit our blunders. You see, pyrotechnics and circus campaigns make great covers for hate. And the colors? They come in handy too: Blue for sadness, white for innocence (lost), and red for blood. *A wrong date? Easy. We'd be happy to do it all over again. No big deal. Two days late. Not needed though.* You won't be forgetting now. Not any time soon. No one can ever forget a girl like Liberty; most likely to succeed. America, land of the free? …America: You got your democracy. **You're fired.**

Warhawk

Eric Nirschel

Washington DC rumbled. Overhead, wings of newly completed F-35s circled the capitol, their pilots scanning the horizon. Below, the treads of M1A2 Abrams Main Battle Tanks wrenched chunks of crumbling asphalt from the roads, supported by groups of Stryker IAVs. Further east of the city, in neighborhoods like Mitchellville, Largo, and Harwood, nervous soldiers dug in, digging trenches and stacking sand bags. Their faces were grim. They were men who were there to do the job.

All eyes lingered on the horizon to the east. Thick, rolling clouds had maintained throughout the day, and as night fell, cold rains came with it. The rain was a mixed blessing. The ice that would surely follow would make it difficult to maintain some of the equipment, and the men were frigid, even in their winter kits. The cold kept them awake, however, and focused on the task at hand. The cloud cover would make the Leviathan stand out on the horizon; the black, writhing shape of that ancient thing would cut stark contrast against the winter gray of the night sky.

Marine 1, the president's personal helicopter, had evacuated the city some hours before, and President Trump could do little but stare listlessly from the window, eyeing the other helicopters in his formation, all identical to the one in which he now sat.

"We'll be setting down momentarily, Mr. President." Stephen Rogers' voice was thin, tense. He'd been Presidential Secretary for less than a year when the Leviathan crisis began, and though he was a skilled bureaucrat, primeval horrors rising from the sea were one of the few things that could take him by surprise.

"Good," Trump replied flatly, "Is it ready?"

"...yes, sir. The Joint Chiefs are waiting to..."

"I don't care what they say. I know the score better than they do. You tell me." President Trump didn't turn away from the window.

"Construction was completed ahead of schedule, and under budget. The gold leaf on the left arm isn't completed, but with time constraints..."

"It'll have to do. We're not gonna get schlonged over some gold leaf, Steve, OK?"

"No sir, I don't believe we will."

The project had been kept secret for three years, until finally the influx of manpower and material to the Lake Ridge facility became impossible for the media to ignore, no matter how many tweets the president sent out. Dubbed the 'Warhawk,' the machine was the greatest weapon of war the world had ever seen. A full 110 tons of steel, titanium alloys, and the most advanced electronic and weapons systems ever developed. Originally a pet project, the Warhawk now served as America's ,and the world's, last hope against the Leviathan. A show was made of choosing its pilot, but the President knew otherwise.

Trump's arrival at the facility was kept quiet; as far as the public knew, he'd been evacuated to a safe house as part of continuity of government contingencies. As the beast bore down on the capitol, all the key players inside the beltway had been evacuated...save one.

The fusion core of the great machine spun up, the entire chassis of the titan deathbringer rattling as if it were about to come apart at the seams. President Trump was unphased. and the mammoth contraption's mountainous frame settled, the core winding down to operational speeds, a faint hum from where he now sat in the cockpit. The radio crackled to life.

"Mr. President, I have to ask again...don't do this. We have pilots. Good pilots, brave men who will pilot the Warhawk, you don't need to..."

"Ya want somethin' done right, sometimes ya just gotta do it yourself, OK? Besides, this nasty monster knocked over my tower, and I don't like that kind of thing, OK?"

There was a long pause, the only sound in the cockpit the sound of 16 inch shells loading into the arm mounted cannons. President Trump engaged the hand actuators, giant titanium gauntlets clenching like fists. He would need those fists.

"The Vice President is here, sir." came Stephen's voice, again weak and thin.

"Mike's there? Put him on."

Another pause.

"You're taking a hell of a risk, Donald. You know that." Pence's voice was firm, unwavering. He knew the President had made up his mind.

"I promised 'em, Mike. I promised my family I'd make America great again. I promised America."

"I know you did, Donald. We both did."

"You promise me, Mike. If I don't come back from this, you..."

"Don't talk like that, Donald. We're going to shock the world." even now, Pence's voice refused to falter. It gave Trump strength.

"Promise."

"America will be great again, Donald."

The two men exchanged no more words. President Trump switched off the coms in the cockpit of the war machine he'd hedged his bets on. Leg servos roared with hydraulic fury, and the earth quaked with the first steps of metal god Trump had built, the presidential seal emblazoned like the battle standard of a great legion on each powerful shoulder. On the horizon, the black shape loomed, the white hot tracer fire of ground forces engaging it illuminating only small portions of its gargantuan monstrosity. The Warhawk marched forward, and as the thunder broke across the sky with a rain of 16 inch shells and hellfire missiles, and the sound of giant titanium alloy punches crushing black, oozing flesh filled the sky, the world watched, breathless and silent. Time stood motionless as the two giants met on that field outside the seat of freedom, and the fate of the world rested in two tiny, tiny hands...

Rat and Miriam

Mark Slade

(Dedicated to David Drake)

"I see those dog-faced assholes now," Miriam screamed as he looked through the periscope and shifted into fifth gear. The tank kicked up a cloud of dust, burying the skeletal dune buggy, baring down on it quickly. The desert sun was high in the sky burning, a hole in old Earth's atmosphere. We were being chased by The State's Imperial police and they were looking to throw Miriam and me in the underground slammer for selling black market oxygen.

Hey, wherever there's a buck to be made, Miriam and me will sell the nipples off a dead bitch's tits.

"Hey Rat," Miriam called out to me. "Those Dick weeds are closing in on us!"

"Go into sixth gear and hit the hyperspeed button," I said. I spun around in my chair, flicked on the necessary switches on the tanks motherboard. The tank wheezed and jittered. The wheels rolled over branches, bushes, a hillside, finally crushing a small house by the sea. We were ready to jump head first in the polluted waters off the coast of Maine when the tank sputtered, choked, died on the shore of rolling waves.

"Fuck!" Miriam cried out. "If they catch us with that oxygen it's over with!" He bawled. Being a mutated hermaphrodite must be hell with those wild mood swings. I'm a woman and my mood swings stay in check at all times. Well, mostly.

"Shut your fucking gob, Miriam!" I screamed at him. He lowered his head, sobbed quietly. "The damned override crossed the lines on the motherboard again. Remind me to give Gav a swift kick in the nuts when I see him."

Gav was our mechanic. I pay him ten percent of the cut from the oxygen I sell to the dead on the streets who still think they are alive. The oxygen goes to their brains and they can function like the rest of us with minimal cannibalism of the living. Minimum, I mean opening their own butcher chops to sell to the living. Oh, the government does not want zombies to become the norm of everyday existence. They wouldn't have a war to wage, thus the world would pay attention to other things fucked up. Such as the water supply being taxed or no regular citizens allowed to have any transportation unless they are a part of the government beat down.

"Get out of your unauthorized vehicle, citizen!" We heard the voice of the police officer. "We will count to three before we commence artillery fallout."

I looked at Miriam. He wiped his eyes and reached for the laser dispenser Gav converted from an Ak-47. I shook my head.

"Let's go out there without those," I said.

"Are you sure, Rat?" He asked, ready to break into tears at any time.

I thought about it, then nodded. "Yeah." I said. "Something tells me the Glorious Ninth can't take any more hits right now."

"AHHHHHHHHHHHH! Stupid tank! Fuck you Gav!" Miriam punched the dashboard. Several 8 track tapes of digital speeches by the former president of the world fell to the tank's floor. Ten years ago Donald J. Trump was gunned down and the military released a virus that killed off most of the population in hopes to rebuild the world with better citizens. Instead, they created a zombie apocalypse that 21st century movies used to cram down our throats.

I motioned for Miriam to open the tank's lid first. He cursed me under his breath.

The lid slid open and Miriam poked his head out. He saw two deputies pointing flash guns at the tank. They all look the same. Those deputies have long spiky pink hair, no shirt under their overalls. Large boils cover their bodies and they have to wear sunglasses because the sun's rays could burn holes in their retinas. I swear the chief of police were cloning these fuckers.

"Get out now!" Deputy 1 screamed.

"Or we'll blast you to kingdom come!" Deputy 2 screamed.

"That's original," I said. "You two are a couple of cards."

I pushed Miriam out of the way so I could pull myself out of the tank. We both lined up against the tank, our backs to them so they can frisk us. I felt hands roll across my breasts and cup my nipples. If I could find clothing less revealing that I could wear in the tank other than a tank top and cargo fatigues, I would.

"Hey! Watch it buddy!" I told one of them. Deputy 1 giggled and snorted. He probably hadn't had any since shore leave, unless he found a willing corpse in a ditch somewhere.

Miriam seemed to enjoy the frisk as well as Deputy 2. He hovered over Miriam, breathing heavily, smiling ear to ear. Miriam wiggled his fat ass to encourage him to do more than touch.

That's when an idea popped in my head.

"You like her?" I said to Deputy 2. He grinned and nodded. "Yeah?" I smiled back. "If you let us go, she will fuck your brains out. How's that, stud?"

The Deputies exchanged glances.

Deputy 2 nodded immediately. Deputy 1 had his doubts.

"The Chief would have our asses for this." He stated. "Zeppo there would be content with a piece of hairy ass and his walking papers. He can always work on his Uncle's pig-shit farm. Me," He jabbed his thumb into his own chest. "I got a family, see. I got four little snot-nosed grubbers, a bartender, and two fucking wives that rely on me. What do I get out of this?"

I sighed heavily and rolled my eyes. I looked over at Miriam, and he and Deputy 2 were already tonguing each other, touching places no one needed to witness. I made up my mind to fake a smile and flutter my eyelashes.

"You know," I made my voice a little more husky and whispery. "I have always wanted to fuck in the Glorious Ninth," I pointed to the tank.

Deputy 1's chest heaved. He shook a bit and stepped closer to me. He laughed, showed me the one good tooth in his jar shaped head. Whatever he'd eaten before did not kill that horrible stench that rose from his rotten gums.

"Let's make hay, baby," Deputy 1 said.

Let's make hay? That was the best that moron could come up with? Pathetic. I smiled at him, took him by the hand. I climbed the thin ladder and watched Deputy 1 follow closely. I climbed down inside the tank slowly. I found a nice dark corner so I couldn't see the nasty fucker's tiny dick. He rushed toward me, tried to plant one on me. I turned my head and giggled.

"Please…let's not rush that part. I like to get right to it," I told him, reached inside his sweaty trousers with my right hand.

"Just my kind of girl," He exhaled and that thing wiggled in my hand before it stiffened. Believe me, I could feel it wasn't impressive.

With my left hand, I found the gas mask connected to one of the tubes of oxygen. "Come here and give me that kiss," I whispered to him. He giggled and pushed his face into mine. I ducked to one side and placed the gas mask on his face. He jerked back slightly, mumbled something inaudible. Before he realized what was happening, I already turned the oxygen lines on. They hissed and popped.

I heard him struggle, began screaming. There was nothing he could do. I turned the knob all the way to ten. Deputy 1 was stuck to the gas mask, his lungs taking in five meters of oxygen. In mere seconds he had lost consciousness. I heard a pop. He fell in the slim sunlight that came from the open hatch of the tank. The gas mask as full of his blood.

I tossed Deputy 1 to the ground before I lowered myself out of the tank. I saw Deputy 2 lying face down, the top of his head had been melted by his own flash gun that Miriam had in belt.

"I see you scored, too," I said.

Miriam had a satisfied look on his peeked face. "You don't know half the story, sister," He smiled sheepishly.

"C'mon, you shit-picker," I yelled at him and climbed in the dune buggy. Miriam sat in the seat behind me, found a pair of goggles. "That fucker Gav can come out here and kick start the Glorious Ninth!"

With that we sped away in a whirlwind from the shores of Maine and headed toward Old Boston, leaving behind us two dead State Imperial Police officers and cloud of black dust.

Coming February

Tainted Love. Lots of sizzling, dark, twisted erotica. An issue that you would not want your parents catch you reading.

Made in the USA
Monee, IL
28 July 2020